Healthy Living

Fruits

by Vanessa Black

Bullfrog Books

Ideas for Parents and Teachers

Bullfrog Books let children practice reading informational text at the earliest reading levels. Repetition, familiar words, and photo labels support early readers.

Before Reading

- Discuss the cover photo. What does it tell them?
- Look at the picture glossary together. Read and discuss the words.

Read the Book

- "Walk" through the book and look at the photos. Let the child ask questions. Point out the photo labels.
- Read the book to the child, or have him or her read independently.

After Reading

- Prompt the child to think more. Ask: How many servings of fruit do you think you eat a day? What is your favorite fruit?

Bullfrog Books are published by Jump!
5357 Penn Avenue South
Minneapolis, MN 55419
www.jumplibrary.com

Library of Congress Cataloging-in-Publication Data

Names: Black, Vanessa, author.
Title: Fruits / by Vanessa Black.
Description: Minneapolis, MN: Jump!, Inc. [2016]
Series: Healthy living | "Bullfrog Books are published by Jump!" | Audience: Ages 5–8.
Audience: K to grade 3.
Includes bibliographical references and index.
Identifiers: LCCN 2016028289 (print)
LCCN 2016029218 (ebook)
ISBN 9781620315446 (hardcover: alk. paper)
ISBN 9781620315798 (pbk.)
ISBN 9781624964923 (ebook)
Subjects: LCSH: Fruit in human nutrition—Juvenile literature. | Fruit—Juvenile literature. | Nutrition—Juvenile literature. | Health—Juvenile literature.
Classification: LCC QP144.F78 B53 2016 (print)
LCC QP144.F78 (ebook) | DDC 641.3/4—dc23
LC record available at https://lccn.loc.gov/201602828

Editor: Jenny Fretland VanVoorst
Book Designer: Molly Ballanger
Photo Researcher: Molly Ballanger

Photo Credits: All photos by Shutterstock except: Getty, 10–11, 14–15, 16, 20–21, 23tr.

Table of Contents

Many Kinds

It is time to start the day.

Rex drinks fruit juice.

Nan eats a fig.

Yum!

Fruit tastes good.
It is good for you, too.

Jed has a kiwi.

Meg eats a melon.

These fruits have vitamin C.
It helps fight colds.

Ty has an orange.
Pia eats a banana.
These fruits have folate.
It helps your blood.

Rae has a mango.
Bai eats an apple.

These fruits have fiber.
It helps you digest.

vine
grapes

Fruit grows on plants.

Grapes grow on vines.

Plums grow on trees.

plum

blueberry
bush

Berries grow on bushes.

Do you like fruit?

There are many kinds.

Try them all! Yum!

Your Daily Fruits

You need three to four servings of fruit a day.

Picture Glossary

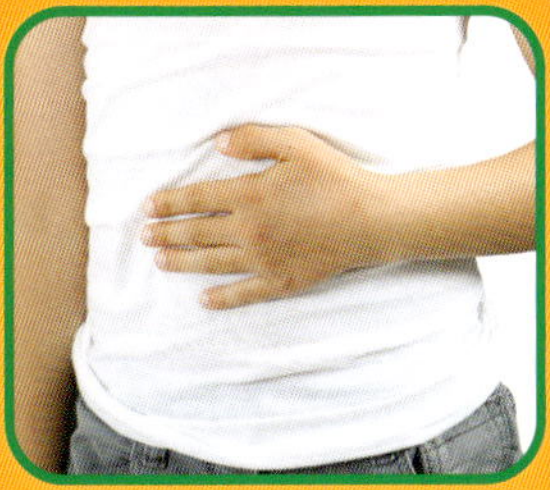

digest
When your body changes food into things your body needs to work properly.

folate
A vitamin that helps your body form red blood cells.

fiber
The part of a food that can't be digested.

vitamin C
A chemical found in fruits that helps protect the body's cells from damage.

Index

To Learn More

Learning more is as easy as 1, 2, 3.

1) Go to www.factsurfer.com

2) Enter "fruits" into the search box.

3) Click the "Surf" button to see a list of websites.

With factsurfer.com, finding more information is just a click away.